D1438638

THE RETURN OF THE
WITCH-DOCTOR

BRACKEN BOOKS No. 13

THE RETURN OF THE WITCH-DOCTOR

by

AMBROSE HAYNES

VICTORY PRESS

LONDON

First published 1957

*Printed in Great Britain by Richard Clay and Company, Ltd.,
Bungay, Suffolk*

CHAPTER ONE

FOR an hour the drums had been throbbing out their strange, insistent message from the jungle. There were pauses when the staccato beats were almost a whisper, and then followed rising surges of sound which beat painfully on the eardrums.

Michael Jameson lay on a camp-bed in the Mission house, listening and wondering what was happening. He had always spent his holidays in the native village of Filembu, hidden deep in the African jungle, with his father and mother, who were medical missionaries, but never had he heard this throbbing of the drums. There was something evil about the sound that made him feel scared and wish he were not alone.

He leaned out of the window and peered out. The white-washed walls of the Mission church and the hospital gleamed against the black pall of the African night. Dim lights from the wood-fires flickered out of the window-openings of the mud huts of the villagers. But there was no sound, only the echoing beat of the drums from the jungle which imprisoned the village on all sides.

"Mensa ! Mensa !" he called out at last.

He had to wait several minutes before an African boy whose face glistened in the light from the oil lamp crept into the room.

"You called, Master Michael," he muttered.

5

"Yes, Mensa. The drums—what do they mean?"

The boy rolled his big, brown eyes and Michael could see that he was shivering with fright.

"Magic, Master Michael. Bad magic. My father go. All men go." He pointed to the jungle.

"But what do you mean, Mensa?" Michael asked. "There's no such thing as magic. Haven't my father and mother been teaching you for a long time about God who loves us all and told us never to be frightened?"

Mensa shrugged. "The God of the white man live long way away," he muttered between chattering teeth. "Magic of the black man here—out there." He pointed to the jungle again. "Kikembu—he come."

"Kikembu——" Michael began to ask a question, but Mensa, with a whimper of fear, scuttled off to the kitchen at the back of the Mission house.

Still the drums throbbed out monotonously. Black man's magic! What could Mensa mean? Michael wished desperately that his father and mother were there. He felt uneasy that this should be happening immediately after their sudden call to Goez, a village some ten miles distant in the jungle. Two days they had been gone now, and as Michael began to think about it, he remembered that the men of the village had been standing about in groups all day, whispering.

He hadn't taken much notice, knowing that this was the dry season, when little work could be done in the rice-fields, but now he began to wonder whether their talk had had something to do with this Kikembu of whom Mensa had appeared to be so frightened.

At fourteen years of age, Michael was tall and strong,

6

with a mop of fair hair. He had already decided that with God's help he too would be a missionary like his father and mother. He was training in a college in Freetown, the capital of Sierra Leone.

If there was trouble brewing in Filembu—and the beating of the drums and Mensa's obvious fear were sure indications—then he must do what he could, he decided. And there was only one person he could go to for help—Bembi, the old chief.

He hurried out of the Mission house, along the beaten mud path, passing the silent huts of the village, until he came to a larger hut with mud walls and a roof of thatched palm-leaves in the shape of a cone.

He pushed aside the loose covering of the door and stepped inside. Bembi sat in his chief's chair, a red fez on his grey head and a loose, white robe about his tall, thin frame. The light from a wood-fire flickered on his black, wrinkled face.

He was staring at the glowing embers, and did not look up as Michael entered.

"You come, Master Michael," he said in a deep, musical voice. "I've expected you. Listen." He held up his hand. "The drums—they call my children."

"What does it mean?" Michael asked, and knelt down beside the chief's chair. "It's been going on for over an hour. I'm a bit scared."

Bembi sighed and placed his hand on Michael's head.

"No good, my son, no good. You are young. Listen as I tell you about my people, the Gzendis."

Michael settled himself on the rush mat before the wood-fire. He knew he would have to be patient, for

Bembi, like all his tribe, was slow in coming to the point. The old chief stared vacantly into the wood-fire for several seconds whilst the drums thundered their sinister message into the dark, silent night.

"Many, many years the Gzendis live here in the forest, my son," Bembi began slowly, nodding his wizened head. "The forest is dark and dangerous and all the time creep towards our little village. We have been taught, my son, to believe that the spirits live in the forest."

"What sort of spirits?" Michael asked.

"Spirits of the trees, of animals, of the dead. Who shall say who they be?" The old man shook his head. "They live there and would devour us. The white man does not understand. The black man—he know."

"But you don't believe that now?" Michael inquired quietly. "You're a Christian now."

The chief's brown eyes lighted up. "Ah, yes, my son, Bembi is a Christian. Your father and mother have taught me about Jesus who drove away the evil spirits and showed men the way to God. Ah, yes, Bembi, he is a Christian all right. He believe, but my people—ah, my people——"

"Tell me, chief Bembi, what are they doing out there in the jungle?" Michael demanded, barely able to control his impatience.

"Listen, my son." The old man smiled a little. "The drums, they beat for the spirits. Kikembu, he is there. He will call up the spirits. They will do as he wishes."

Michael felt a cold shiver run down his spine. The drums were beating out with a slow, monotonous rhythm which, after Bembi's explanation, made the dark African night seem more sinister than ever.

"But it can't be true, Bembi," Michael jerked out. "There aren't evil spirits. The Gzendis can't believe that."

"Who can say?" the chief murmured slowly. "Your father and mother, they good people. They teach much and always the Gzendis listen, but always there is the forest, and now Kikembu, he come."

The way he said that implied that nothing more need be said.

"Chief Bembi," Michael demanded, "who is this Kikembu? Are you afraid of him as Mensa, our house-boy, is and as it seems all the tribe are? Who is he? Where does he come from?"

The old chief rose slowly from his chair, went over into a dark corner of the hut and returned to the fire-light, carrying a long-handled spear. Despite his age, he was an impressive sight as he drew himself up to his full height.

"I am Bembi, chief of the Gzendis," he thundered and drove the spear into the ground. "I have been the greatest warrior for miles. I, Bembi, fear no man."

"You *are* afraid of Kikembu." Michael insisted bravely. He jumped to his feet and faced the old warrior. "Why are you afraid?"

Slowly the chief's figure bent and the fire went out of his eyes. He groped for a chair and slumped down.

"Yes, my son, you have guessed right," he admitted in a tired voice. "I, Bembi, am afraid too of Kikembu, the great witch-doctor. And only to you do I say it. He come from Goez——"

9

"That is where mother and father have gone," Michael gasped. "I don't understand."

The old chief nodded wearily. "Kikembu, he come yesterday. He tell us the God of the white men no good. He say your father and mother never come back. He say the spirits of the jungle have taken them away——"

"But, chief Bembi, you can't believe that. You know they were called for because there was an outbreak of fever in Goez." Michael cried out in sudden alarm. "That's true, isn't it, Bembi? It's true, isn't it? Nothing has happened to my father and mother, has it?"

The old man shook his head wearily. "Who knows?" he moaned. "But Kikembu come and say these things. He is a great witch-doctor. Tonight he make rain. Then everybody will be sure that he speak the truth."

Michael was feeling desperate. An uneasy fear grew in his mind that something had happened to his father and mother and that the witch-doctor was responsible. It didn't help matters to realise that even Bembi was afraid—and that he was alone.

"Look here, chief Bembi," he pleaded. "You keep on talking in riddles. Can't you tell me everything? Aren't you a Christian? Aren't you our friend any more?"

"Your friend, my son?" Bembi repeated. "Yes, always your friend. But when Kikembu come he bring things I cannot answer. The rains come late this year. The rice-fields are dry and scorched. If no rain come, then the Gzendis go hungry. It is a bad thing to be hungry, my son. Now Kikembu say he make rain and the rice will grow and the Gzendis will have plenty to eat. So, he say, the Gzendis must not speak to the white

10

man's God any more. He say the spirits are angry with the Gzendis. Tonight Kikembu make rain."

"So that's it," Michael gasped.

Often had he heard his father talk of the superstitions of the Africans and the power that the witch-doctor wielded before the missionaries came. And he knew that his father had been concerned about the length of the dry season which threatened the crop from the rice-fields.

So this Kikembu was using the drought to undermine the faith of the Gzendis and to try to get back his power, Michael reasoned. A very real fear that something terrible was happening came to him.

"Bembi, chief of the Gzendis," Michael pleaded. "You've got to help. You can't let Kikembu get away with it. Supposing my father and mother are in danger. Supposing"—he didn't dare to put into words the thoughts that ran through his mind—"Bembi, you've got to help."

The old chief drew his robes about him and stared into the wood-fire. His black, wizened face was full of sadness and there was fear in his brown eyes.

"We must wait, my son," he muttered slowly. "Your father and mother I love. They do much for the Gzendis and they teach me about God. But Kikembu is a great witch-doctor. If he make rain——" He broke off and shrugged. "I, Bembi, can do nothing then."

Michael stared at the old man. He just couldn't believe that this chief who had been the first convert at the Mission and so great a friend of his father and mother could sit there and do nothing. Yet things that he had been told helped to explain.

11

He remembered his father had once said, "One day, Michael, you too will be a missionary, I trust. Then you will understand that these people are like children. They have been taught for generations to believe in spirits and magic. We have got to show them that the love of God is greater than all that. Never judge them too hardly, Michael. Try to understand."

Michael stood upright before Bembi.

"Look, I'm going out to the jungle," he declared. "There I will talk to this Kikembu. I'll ask him what has happened to my father and mother and I'll tell him that he must leave the Gzendis alone."

At that, the chief looked up, started and lifted a trembling hand in protest.

"No, my son, no," he protested. "Kikembu will kill you. You must not go. I, Bembi, command you. What can you, a boy, do against the magic of Kikembu? No, my son, it is too dangerous."

"I don't know what I can do," Michael confessed, and his face was white and strained in the flickering light of the wood-fire. "But I shan't go alone into the jungle to face Kikembu. God will be with me and will show me what to do. Bembi, please come too. Haven't my father and mother taught you that God will always help you when you are in danger?"

He broke off as a sudden scuffle at the doorway opening distracted his attention. A small, dark figure hurtled into the hut and fell at Michael's feet.

"Mensa!" Michael gasped. "What's the matter?"

"For you, Master Michael." The African boy panted. He was shaking and his brown eyes were bright with fear. "A man come to Mission. He say give you this."

Michael took the small parcel wrapped in palm leaves from the boy's trembling hands. Quickly he unfolded it and held up a khaki shirt.

"What's this?" he exclaimed in surprise, and then gave a shudder as he saw the dark brown patch on the shoulder. "It's my father's!" he gasped. "And it's bloodstained. Oh, Bembi, look! What have they done to my father and mother? Bembi—look!"

The old chief rose from his chair slowly and took the shirt in his hands. He shook his head sadly.

"Bad business, my son," he muttered. "This is a message from Kikembu, but what it means, who knows?"

"We have got to find out," Michael pleaded, for now his worst fears seemed to be confirmed. "He has done something to them. Oh, Bembi, you must help me. You must. There's nobody else."

For a long time the chief stood, staring into the smouldering fire. Then, suddenly, he braced his shoulders.

"I am Bembi, chief of the Gzendis," he declared. "We go to Kikembu. But first you, my son, will talk to the Good God, for, in my heart, I am afraid, and without His help I cannot go."

"Thanks, Bembi," Michael replied gratefully. "I will pray as you ask, and will you take this?" He handed his old friend a New Testament which, many years ago, his father had translated into the Gzendis dialect. "That's better than all Kikembu's magic."

Then, reverently, he knelt down beside him on the earth-floor. What was before them in the dark jungle he did not know. He could only guess at what might

13

have happened to his father and mother. There was only one thing of which he could be sure. God would be with him and the old chief, and help them. Thus he put his life into God's care, and when he rose from his knees he was strengthened.

CHAPTER TWO

WHEN Mensa had discovered the intention of Michael and Bembi, he scuttled back in fear to the Mission house and bolted all the doors.

Bembi threw the corner of his white robe over his shoulder and led the way into the darkness. Despite his age, there was a dignity about the way he held his head high, and Michael, following him, had the thought flash through his mind that it must have been thus that the old warrior had many years ago led his tribe into battle.

Without a word they passed through the rice-fields, guided towards the tangled, black mass of the jungle by the throbbing of the drums. In his hand Bembi carried the small Testament, and every now and again Michael could hear him mumbling a few words to himself. He knew then that the old chief was still afraid, and as they neared what seemed to be an impenetrable wall of towering trees, Bembi faltered.

"Go on, Bembi," Michael urged in a whisper. "We must go on."

The old man sighed and nodded his head. "Keep close to me, my son," he murmured. "Inside it is as black as Kikembu's heart."

The African jungle swallowed them. Bembi stalked stealthily through the elephant grass which was taller than his head, through the tangled, treacherous undergrowth, with the inborn instinct of a native. Michael

15

could only stumble after him, his main purpose to keep in touch. From overhead came the occasional chatter of monkeys as Michael's clumsy progress disturbed their rest. And all the time the throbbing of the drums came clearer.

Once in that dark trek through the jungle, Bembi stopped and grasped Michael's arm.

"Quiet, my son, listen!" he whispered.

Michael heard it clearly. The soft swish of a furry skin brushing against the bark of a tree.

"Leopard." Bembi grunted. "It is good that the wind is against him. Otherwise he smell us."

Michael shivered. He'd never been in the jungle at night before, but he knew that the marauding leopard was to be feared above all animals of the jungle.

"Lay still, my son, listen. Now he is gone. We go forward." Bembi murmured. It was almost as though he could see through the inky blackness.

Suddenly the beating of the drums stopped and the jungle was quiet except for the scurrying sounds of night-prowling animals.

"Kikembu start his magic," Bembi said, but did not hesitate in his stealthy march through the tangled undergrowth.

Five minutes more of plodding, and then Bembi held Michael's arm firmly again.

"Quiet now, my son," he whispered. "We come to the place."

He bent down and crawled forward on his hands and knees. Michael followed, hardly daring to breath. Bembi carefully parted the tall elephant grass with his hands.

16

"See, my son," he whispered.

Michael gasped.

Before them was a clearing in the jungle. A great fire blazed in the centre, and round it sat the men of the village of Filembu. Michael could recognise their black faces glistening in the red glare of the fire. There was Gezi, dressed in a white robe and the bowler hat on his head of which he was so proud. And Felindi and Baluki and many others. All came to the Mission church and sang hymns on Sundays with great gusto—especially Baluki, who was fat and jovial. Now they sat silent, their faces tense, their attention riveted on the tall figure who danced with great loping steps around the fire.

This must be Kikembu, Michael thought. He had a terrifying appearance, this witch-doctor. Over his head was a great wooden mask, his black, glistening body was bare except for a loin-cloth and his breast and arms were painted in streaks of red.

He pranced and loped round the fire, waving his arms rhythmically towards the sky and then down to an earthenware pot on the ground.

This went on for several minutes and, despite his anxiety and fears, Michael lay on the grass numbed by the awe-inspiring spectacle of Kikembu dancing in the red glare of the fire surrounded by the black tangle of the African jungle.

Bembi was silent too. He remembered all the things that he had been taught as a boy about witch-doctors; of their power to summon evil spirits; of how they could kill a man by magic spells. In the darkness of the night he again half believed all these things and was afraid.

17

They watched as Kikembu in a great flurry of a dance, flung himself to the ground, then rose slowly and, imitating the graceful stride of a leopard, walked on all fours round the circle of natives, casting, as he pretended, a spell upon them.

Baluki's brown eyes were rolling with fear in his fat face. Michael could see that, and was suddenly very sorry for Baluki and all the others who knew no better than to be frightened by this terrifying Kikembu.

After he had made a complete circle, the witch-doctor took from a pouch in his loin-cloth a handful of stones. With a great gesture these he threw into the earthenware pot and then taking a bamboo stick from the ground he waved it towards the sky and then down to the pot.

"Kikembu make rain." Bembi muttered in a trembling whisper. "Kikembu, great witch-doctor. To-morrow it rain, then the rice grow and everybody know how great Kikembu is."

"But that's ridiculous," Michael burst out. Suddenly the spell that the weird sight had cast over him was gone. "How can he make rain fall by just waving a stick at the clouds? You don't believe the clouds take any notice of Kikembu, do you?"

Bembi ignored the question. "Kikembu, great witch-doctor," was all he would mutter and his eyes were fixed, as though he were mesmerised, on the gesticulating magician.

"Look, Bembi," Michael declared. "I'm going out there to talk to Kikembu. I'm not frightened any more. Jesus was good and kind and didn't frighten people like

18

this, and He is with us, Bembi. He will take care of us."

"No—no—my son," Bembi cried out. "You do not understand. If you go now, Kikembu will kill you."

"If you won't come with me, then I'll go alone," Michael insisted desperately. "Something has happened to my father and mother and that witch-doctor is at the bottom of it. Baluki and all the rest of them *can't* let him do what he likes—they can't—Bembi——"

"No—no——" the old chief cried out. "Michael, my son—come back—come back——"

But Michael had stepped out from the tangled undergrowth and was walking slowly into the clearing. He felt scared now as he approached the circle of Africans, but he prayed desperately for strength.

Not until he came within the glare of the fire did Kikembu notice him. Then, looking straight at him, the witch-doctor dropped his wand and with loping strides broke through the circle of men. His head nodding and chanting, Michael knew not what incantations, the witch-doctor led him into the circle.

Close up, Kikembu looked even more terrifying. The mask over his head had a horrible grin and the big, wooden eyes glared evilly. A cry of surprise came from the natives, but no one moved. Michael knew then that he was alone, at the mercy of the witch-doctor. Even Bembi seemed to have deserted him. It was an awful moment, yet, as he prayed, he knew that he was not alone.

Placing Michael close to the fire, the witch-doctor began a slow, weird dance around him. Michael tried to protest, not knowing what evil designs Kikembu had in

19

his mind, but the black, leaping figure appeared not to understand a word. All sorts of stories that he had read ran through Michael's mind, yet he stood still. He knew that he must not show any fear. But how would it end?

"Michael, my son. Bembi, he come!"

The strangled cry startled Kikembu, and he stood stock still watching the old chief stumble into the circle and place his arm about his victim.

"I was afraid," Bembi whispered. "Then I watched. I saw you stand before Kikembu, the great witch-doctor, and I was not afraid any more. I know that the white man's God is my God too—and I come."

He drew himself upright, a noble figure in the dancing firelight.

"I, Bembi, chief of the Gzendis," he commanded in the local dialect, "tell you to go from Filembu and leave my people in peace, Kikembu. They have found the true God and will only worship Him."

There were murmurs from the seated Gzendis and they whispered to one another. Michael knew then that they loved their old chief. But would their fear of Kikembu be the greater?

The witch-doctor quickly put the matter to the test. He stood before Bembi, twirled and danced in a fantastic series of acrobatic movements, and then came to a sudden stop and addressed the old chief in a high-pitched voice.

"What does he say, Bembi," Michael asked.

"He say the witch-doctor return to Filembu. He say too long we desert the old gods. He say tomorrow it will rain, then we all understand. He say he take the white man and woman away and punish them. He say

20

you must go away. And he say, my son, that I must die
—I, Bembi, chief of the Gzendis, must die because I
stand before him.''

"No, Bembi, no," Michael cried. "You mustn't let
him get away with it. He can do nothing to you. Look,
you have the Testament in your hand. That is stronger
than all Kikembu's curses. Bembi, listen to me. Talk
to your people. Make them understand."

The old man nodded his head. "You are right, my
son," he said slowly.

He brushed the witch-doctor aside with his arm and
spoke gently to his people.

"Once we believed in the things that Kikembu would
have us believe," he told them in their native tongue,
"but the missionaries came and taught us about the
God who lives in the Heavens and sent His Son, Jesus,
into the world to take away our fears and who was
killed so that we might be forgiven for all the evil things
that the witch-doctors taught us to do and so that one
day we might go to live with God in Heaven.

"Since then, my Gzendis, we have lived in peace.
We have put away our spears and the good missionaries
have built the school in which to teach our children,
and the hospital to tend our sick. These have been good
days for the Gzendis.

"And now Kikembu has come and would wish us to
go back to the evil days. He would make us forsake the
God who loves us. He would kill that Jesus again and
we would be lost.

"Oh, my Gzendis, for a time I, too, was afraid. Then
this boy reminded me of the Book"—he held up the
Testament—"and you remember how our good friends,

21

the missionaries, have read from it in the chapel every Sunday. This boy, too, faced Kikembu alone—Kikembu, who is evil and has spirited away the good missionaries."

"My friends"—his voice rose passionately—"I am no longer afraid. Bembi will face Kikembu, too, and tell him that his ways are evil. Come, my friends, let us go back to our homes at Filembu, but first let us demand of Kikembu what he has done with our good friends."

He glanced proudly and confidently around at the seated Gzendis. Michael, although he had understood only a little, could see that Bembi's address had impressed them and they were uneasy. Gezi, a thin-faced, quiet man, who kept a number of pets, whispered into the ear of Baluki, and then rose to his feet. Slowly he walked across to Bembi and gave the greeting, "Isser." More slowly, Baluki struggled up and waddled across. "Isser," he muttered, and there were beads of perspiration on his fat face.

But no other man moved. They stared sullenly at Kikembu, and Michael knew then that the battle was lost for the time being.

The witch-doctor again performed his weird dance, and this time his hands moved not towards the earthenware pot, but towards the four who stood alone in the centre.

"We must go, my son," Bembi whispered. "And I say it this time not because I am afraid, but because Kikembu has spread his magic on my people and we shall find no help here. We must wait until tomorrow and then—who knows?—maybe the Gzendis will be

22

men again and then we can do something with Kikembu
and find your father and mother. I am sorry, my son.
I, Bembi, have spoken."

Michael nodded his head. He felt sad, miserable and
terribly anxious. Yet he knew that the old chief had
spoken the truth. There were only four of them, and
they could do nothing against the rest.

Slowly, with Bembi leading the way, they left the
circle of men and plodded into the black jungle. Behind them they could hear the maniacal shrieks and
laughter of Kikembu.

The witch-doctor had indeed returned to the
Gzendis!

CHAPTER THREE

THERE was little sleep for the four that night. After they left the clearing, Bembi led them back to his hut. There he sat in his chief's chair, whilst Gezi and Baluki and Michael squatted on rush mats before him. They said nothing for a long time, each busy with his sad thoughts.

Michael studied his new friends as the light from the wood-fire flickered over their black faces. Gezi's thin face was strained, and the bowler hat—which he wore proudly as a sign of civilisation—did not detract from the dignity of his thin, tall frame.

Baluki, on the other hand, was quite obviously frightened, and beads of perspiration glistened on his fat face. Occasionally he drew his red robe tighter around his enormous body and shivered.

At last Bembi broke the silence.

"I speak slowly in the white man's tongue," he said, "because you, Gezi, and you, Baluki, speak it not much."

The two Africans nodded their heads.

"Kikembu bad man, but good witch-doctor. To-morrow, or the day after, it rain, and then the Gzendis will believe him."

"How can Kikembu make it rain?" Michael demanded. "We've said it before that he can't."

Bembi smiled slowly and wisely and shook his wizened, old head.

24

"My son," he replied, "there are many things I do not understand about witch-doctors, but this I do know. They study the heavens and know the signs."

"Got it!" gasped Michael. "You mean they study the weather. It's like we say, 'Red sky at night, shepherd's delight, red sky in the morning, shepherd's warning'."

The old chief nodded his head and smiled whimsically. "Yes, my son," he said. "This Kikembu has seen the signs in the sky, and he know it will rain soon. So he come and pretend to make rain——"

"Then everybody will believe he brought it!" Michael exclaimed. "Gracious! Can't they see through his tricks?"

Gezi spread his thin hands over the fire. "You see tonight. Kikembu clever. Even me believe for time," he murmured in a slow, musical voice.

Michael nodded his head. Yes, he could understand. The witch-doctor had a way with him that impressed you, and Michael had to remember that the Gzendis had been brought up to fear him.

"We have to decide what we do," Bembi broke in solemnly. "We can wait and see what happen. Then Kikembu may try to kill us. We can go into the jungle and wait there. Perhaps Kikembu fail, and then we come back——"

"We've got to do something about father and mother," Michael urged desperately.

"We go jungle—quick." Baluki mumbled and started to struggle to his feet. His first act of strength in defying the witch-doctor was now behind him, and he was mortally afraid.

25

"No, Baluki." Michael jumped to his feet. "We must stop here and see it out. If we lose touch with Kikembu, then we shall lose all chance of finding out where my father and mother are. Don't you see that Kikembu wants us out of the way? When we are gone, he can do what he likes with the Gzendis. What do you say, Gezi?"

The African looked at Michael steadily and then his lips curled slowly into a smile. "You brave boy. We stop," he said.

"I, Bembi, say we stop too."

Baluki flopped down on to the mat. His big brown eyes rolled with fear. But he said no more.

"I'm glad," Michael sighed. "We may be in danger tomorrow, as you said, Baluki, but God will protect us and look after us. You must believe that. Kikembu must not make you afraid again."

"Perhaps, my son," Bembi murmured. "You will pray for us."

"I'll try," Michael replied quietly.

As he knelt down he knew that this was the most important prayer of his life. The black African night was still. There was but the flickering light of the wood-fire inside the hut. Out there in the dark, forbidding jungle were the Gzendis, overwhelmed by the evil incantations of Kikembu. And somewhere his father and mother were in danger—or dead.

"Lord Jesus," he prayed, "be near to us and keep us safe. And give us faith so that we are not afraid of Kikembu. Especially do Thou help Bembi and Gezi and Baluki, for they have been brought up to believe in evil spirits. And, please Jesus, take care of my father and mother and show me how I may help to bring them out of danger. Amen.''

He was in a strange country and in' dangerous circumstances, but Michael felt, as he prayed, the presence of Jesus, and he was no longer afraid. Bembi and Gezi, and even Baluki, must have felt it too, for they sat back, strangely quiet and calm—to wait.

The first streak of dawn slashed across the black sky, and suddenly there were the insistent cries and yells of the wild animals and birds from the jungle as they awakened to the day's hunting and ceaseless search for food. In minutes almost the black pall of night was gone and bright sunlight filtered through the window opening of the hut. The night's vigil was over. The four looked at one another with calm resignation, waiting for whatever might happen. Even Baluki had stilled his trembling.

They did not have long to wait.

They heard the sound of high-pitched singing coming from the edge of the jungle. They went to the door opening and saw Kikembu, still looking strange and weird in the bright sunlight as, dancing and leaping in the air, he led the Gzendis towards the village.

The womenfolk and children, who during the night had not stirred from their huts, now appeared for fleeting moments and then scuttled back indoors. They did not know what was happening and were too frightened to want to find out.

Swaying and dancing, Kikembu led the Africans to the doorway of Bembi's hut. There he halted and held up his hand.

Bembi stepped forward, dignified and unafraid.

27

"I do not know what evil you have worked on my people, Kikembu," he declared in the native dialect. "But now, in the name of the God whom I have learned to love and serve, I beg you to go and leave us in peace."

The witch-doctor drew himself up to his full height. He was taller than Bembi and, with the hideous, wooden mask over his head, he looked terrifying. He said nothing, but, stepping forward, placed four small wooden models of men on the ground. Then he waved his hands solemnly and murmured some strange incantations.

The Gzendis hedged backwards from the mumbling witch-doctor. Bembi and Gezi started visibly, whilst Baluki, all his calm deserting him, fell down on the ground, grovelling with fear.

"Bembi, Bembi. What's happening?" Michael whispered.

Bembi looked down at him and his wrinkled face was grim. "It means death, my son," he murmured. "Kikembu has put a curse on us. These four models are us. He has cursed them, and we shall die in two days."

Michael nodded his head. He had heard of this kind of thing from his father. Sometimes the model was pierced through the heart with an arrow or shattered with a spear. Then the person, according to the curse, must die. And die they often did—not from the curse, but from fear. Fear—yes, that was Kikembu's strongest magic over these simple people.

And Michael wasn't afraid. He offered a quick prayer for strength and then stepped boldly forward and stood before Kikembu. He said not a word. His face grim and

28

set, he picked up the wooden models and held them above his head so that all could see.

Then he spoke.

"Listen, Gzendis," he cried out. "These are only pieces of wood, and Kikembu is trying to make you believe that with them he can kill Bembi and Gezi and Baluki. My father and mother have taught you that these things are not true, that if you will only trust in God He will deliver you from fear. Look, I will show you——"

Perhaps they only understood a little of what he said, but the Gzendis were hushed with awe. Before the wondering gaze of them all, Michael took out a notebook from his pocket, tore out a few pages and crumpled them. Then he placed the paper on the ground and carefully stacked the pieces of wood over it. He struck a match. The paper flared and the wood, being tinder dry, began to smoke and then blaze.

Gasps of astonishment greeted his action. It was probably more the confident air with which Michael did this than his actual work which impressed them. The Gzendis crowded forward to see this sight, and in their eagerness even pushed Kikembu aside. Bembi's arm went about Michael's shoulders.

"Thank you, my son," he whispered. "For a moment even I was afraid again. Look at my people."

Michael glanced round. He had always known the Gzendis as a happy, carefree people, easily pleased and quick to laugh. That was why the scene in the jungle the night before had so shocked him.

And now the Gzendis were laughing. Their black faces were wreathed in smiles. Michael's spontaneous action in defying the witch-doctor and making him look silly before them had had an effect that he had not anticipated. For the moment their fear of Kikembu was gone. They crowded round Michael, a little shame-faced, but friendly again. Kikembu threw himself on the ground, writhing and groaning with anger.

The wooden models blazed merrily now and a thin spiral of smoke rose gently upwards. Michael sighed. Everything was going to be all right. He was glad he hadn't been afraid. He raised his head to the sky.

"Thank you, Lord Jesus, for giving me courage," he prayed.

Then—just when everything seemed to be turning in his favour—he felt the heavy drops of rain on his head. A dark cloud passed across the sun, casting a black shadow over the group standing there. In a few seconds rain fell in a deluge. The small fire spluttered and died.

A great gasp of astonishment burst from the throats of the Gzendis. The smiles were wiped from their faces, to be replaced by awe and fear. Kikembu, immensely clever and understanding in the ways of the Africans, saw this as a great opportunity and seized it.

He towered before them, awe-inspiring in his wooden mask and the daubs of red paint on his body. He pointed upwards to the cloud, spread his hands and waved them towards the smouldering fire.

There was no need for Michael to be able to under-stand his dialect to know what he was saying. He had brought the rain as he had promised, and their crops of rice would flourish. Not only that, but he had brought the rain at that very moment to show the

Gzendis that he had the power to put out the white boy's fire.

"See." His waving hands seemed to say. "He defied the witch-doctor's spell of death, but I"—he beat his hands on his breast—"am greater than he. Am I not Kikembu, the great witch-doctor, with power over the rain and of life and death?"

It was all a coincidence—Michael knew that. He remembered what Bembi had told him of the weather-lore of the witch-doctors. But would the Gzendis believe that?

He looked round at them, and knew that this, more than anything else, had convinced them of the power of Kikembu.

And what of his friends? Would they believe the witch-doctor too? There were looks of dismay and bewilderment on the old chief's and Gezi's faces, but whether they believed Kikembu, Michael couldn't tell. Baluki, however, couldn't hide the terror from his fat face.

Michael ran towards them.

"I can only guess what Kikembu is telling them," he gasped. "But you don't believe him, Bembi, do you? You mustn't. It's just a coincidence that it started raining——"

Bembi looked down at him, and his wrinkled face was set.

"No, my son, I do not believe," he said. "But it is bad. My people now trust Kikembu. Come, we go into the hut. The rain very bad."

And indeed the rain was now falling in torrents. Michael was soaked to the skin, but he had been so agitated that he had not noticed it. Now he followed Gezi and Baluki into the old chief's hut and huddled with them round the wood-fire.

Outside they could hear Kikembu, still talking to the Gzendis. He was confident now and his voice was shrill and penetrating. The torrential rain did not seem to have any effect on the crowd. They were too much under his spell to care. Nevertheless, after a few minutes Kikembu led them to the palaver house, a large, rectangular building with a roof of thatched palm leaves and open sides.

"They go to decide what they do," Bembi said. "They have much palaver and then—who knows? Kikembu has them in the hollow of his hand."

"Kikembu very powerful," Gezi murmured. "But maybe people not do as he wish. We wait." He gave a slow smile. "I have peace here. I not afraid. Jesus here."

Michael was astounded. Bembi had been afraid and had conquered, and now Gezi, who had been led by the others into the jungle, now had a calm resignation on his thin face which showed clearly that he, too, had conquered. But Baluki said not a word.

"Shall we pray?" Michael ventured to ask, and at a nod from Bembi and Gezi they knelt down on the rush mats.

"Lord Jesus," Michael said, "we are in danger, but we know that Thou are with us. The rain has come, and for the moment Kikembu seems to have won. Yet we know that Thou wilt conquer in the end because Thou dost love us and didst die for us. Thou lovest the Gzendis too, even though they are doing wrong things.

32

Please keep us strong in the faith, no matter what happens, and please take care of my father and mother, wherever they are. Amen."

For a few minutes they still knelt there, feeling the strength of God's power about them, and then they rose.

But now there were only three of them—Baluki had vanished.

CHAPTER FOUR

THIS was the most difficult thing of all—to wait and see what would happen. They talked of Baluki's sudden disappearance, and could only conclude that his bravery in the jungle had deserted him, and that now he had joined the Gzendis in the palaver hut to make his peace with Kikembu.

Bembi, with his deep knowledge of tribal customs, was doubtful whether such an offer by Baluki would be accepted. Kikembu had cast his spell, and Baluki was included in it. Therefore there could be no escape from it, no matter what Baluki might do.

They were sorry for the fat, jovial African, however, and Michael realised afresh how child-like these natives were, how one moment they would be strong and the next weak. Bembi and Gezi seemed to be made of sterner stuff, or was it, despite their wavering at the beginning, that they truly wished to follow in the path of Jesus? He could not be sure of this until the great testing time which he knew must come.

Gezi was quiet, and only joined in the conversation now and again, his knowledge of English being limited. At short intervals, however, he and Bembi spoke to one another in the native dialect, and it was after one of these conversations that Bembi turned to Michael.

"Gezi wishes me to thank you for the example you

have given him," he said slowly. "He say at first he forget God, and then you stood in front of Kikembu and he knew. He say he now has the peace of God and he wish to do something for you. Gezi very fond of animals. He wish to make you a present of one."

Michael flushed with pleasure. In the midst of personal danger and worry about his parents, this kindly thought of Gezi's made him feel pleased, and he smiled his thanks.

"Come, I show," Gezi said, his sharp bright eyes, lighting up.

Michael followed him out of the hut. The village was quiet and deserted. The womenfolk and children had confined themselves indoors. The men were with Kikembu in the palaver house. The torrential rain had stopped as suddenly as it began, but black, thundery clouds warned that the rainy season had arrived and that the downpour was but a prelude to weeks of heavy rain.

It was cool in Gezi's hut. He lived there alone, being a quiet man who seldom liked company. His main interest was his animals.

Two small monkeys scrambled about the place, and as soon as they saw Gezi they jumped on to his shoulder and chattered away delightedly. One even impudently removed Gezi's bowler hat and placed it sideways on his head, much to Michael's amusement.

Half a dozen small tortoises, a baby alligator, a civet cat and a dog. Michael could make out these in the semi-darkness, and also a yellow-breasted parrot perched in the roof, cawing away loudly.

Unperturbed, Gezi fumbled in a corner. He placed in

Michael's hand a small brown animal, soft and warm, something like a squirrel without a tail.

"Mongoose," he smiled. "You like him, eh?"

"Gee, thanks," Michael exclaimed.

The mongoose squinted up at him with bright, shining eyes. Then promptly ran up his arm, down his back and popped into his pocket, where he burrowed for a second or two and then seemed quite at home.

"He make friend." Gezi grinned. "He good. Mongoose very good."

If circumstances had been different, Michael would have enjoyed his visit to Gezi's hut, but danger from the palaver house brooded over them, and they went back to Bembi, still to wait what might be planned. Always there was the hope in their hearts that the Gzendis would come to their senses.

Michael did, however, appreciate the kindness of this solemn-faced, kindly African, and the warmth of the little mongoose against his thigh was a comfort.

They had not long to wait for Kikembu. The witch-doctor had now discarded his wooden mask, and he stood in the doorway to Bembi's hut, a tall, lean man with a wrinkled, evil face. His bloodshot eyes glanced quickly all round the hut. Then, with an impatient wave of the hand, he summoned half a dozen of the Gzendis to him.

They were uneasy, their eyes were downcast, but obviously they were now completely under the power of Kikembu. Silently, without any warning of what they were about to do, they seized Michael, Bembi and Gezi and fastened their legs and arms with ropes. It was useless to resist. There were far too many of them.

36

Bembi's eyes were sad and his wrinkled face looked very old.

"My children, they bind me like a dog," he murmured.

He looked up at Kikembu proudly and spoke in sharp, short sentences. The witch-doctor leered and then gave a high-pitched laugh, pointing to the village. Bembi started as though he had been struck, and he struggled desperately with the ropes binding him. It was no use. The Gzendis had done their work well.

"What did he say? What is he going to do?" Michael asked desperately, for he could see that Bembi was greatly agitated.

"He say he burn down the school and the hospital and the chapel," Bembi groaned. "He say he have no more of the white man's power over the Gzendis. And he will do it, my son. My people are bewitched."

"But he can't! He mustn't!" gasped Michael, and he too struggled desperately with his bonds. "My father and mother have spent years building all this up. Oh, Bembi, what can we do?"

"There is nothing, my son," the old chief sighed. "The witch-doctor has returned, and it is an evil day for the Gzendis."

"What do you think he will do with us?" Michael jerked out.

Bembi sighed again. "He is afraid to harm us openly, I think. He cannot go too far. The white man's officials will come. No, Kikembu is too clever for that. He works by cunning. We must be very careful."

Through the doorway opening they could see Kikembu. Now he was addressing the Gzendis, whipping them up into a frenzy. Michael could hardly believe that the kindly, easy-going Gzendis could be so worked up by one man, but there it all was.

The witch-doctor lighted a branch of a tree dipped in tar. It spluttered and then blazed. Holding it high above his head, dancing and gesticulating wildly, he urged the Gzendis forward, and now they were almost as wild and abandoned as he.

"If only it would rain," Michael exclaimed. "If only it would rain."

Yet, although the black clouds cast their deep shadow over the scene, there was no rain to foil Kikembu's plans. It almost seemed that he really had the uncanny powers he claimed. Michael was not surprised now that the Gzendis believed in his magic.

After that they could but guess what was happening. They could hear yells and shrieks. Michael bit his lip. It was terrible to lie there, helpless, knowing that all his parent's work was being destroyed. If only he could free himself ! He tugged at the ropes round his arm until they bit into his flesh, but it was no good.

Suddenly Kikembu appeared at the doorway. He grinned malevolently and threw on to the mud floor a wicker basket. As quietly as he had come, he disappeared.

Bembi and Gezi glanced quickly at one another.

"Don't move, Michael my son," Bembi whispered urgently. "If we do not move, he may not strike. Yes, Kikembu is truly an evil man."

With fascinated eyes, Michael stared at the wicker basket. It had a lid which had been thrown open by the

38

fall, and slowly a snake, darkish green in colour and about three feet long, slithered its way out.

It raised its evil head and stared fixedly at the three captives. Michael lay there, frozen with horror. So this was Kikembu's plan! To be bitten by a snake would not involve the witch-doctor. It often happened, and Kikembu could easily explain it away as an accident. Oh, how right Bembi had been!

He stared in horror as the snake slithered leisurely towards them. He prayed desperately for help and strength, yet in that moment his faith almost deserted him.

And then he felt a slight stirring in his pocket. Instinctively, the mongoose had scented the danger and smelt the approach of his deadliest enemy.

He pranced out on to the beaten mud floor, a diminutive animal to face such a formidable foe. Yet he was unafraid. He looked almost cheeky as he faced the enemy. The snake raised its head. It struck like quicksilver. Yet the mongoose was even faster, and darted to one side.

Now began the strangest game before Michael's fascinated eyes. To and fro the mongoose darted, always just that much faster than the snake's striking head. It was a game that the mongoose seemed he could keep up for ever. To and fro, to and fro he darted— so fast that the eye could hardly follow him.

And slowly the snake tired. The striking head slowed. The snake seemed to despair of ever catching this darting, little animal—and hesitated.

In a split second, quick as lightning, the mongoose leapt at the head of the snake. In a few seconds it was all over. The snake writhed, and then lay inert on the floor.

Just as though this were all in a day's work, the mongoose slipped over to Michael, burrowed into his pocket and went to sleep.

"Gee!" gasped Michael. "What an escape!"

Gezi's eyes were bright. He nodded his head. "Mongoose good little fellow."

But Bembi's eyes were fast closed and his lips moved in prayer.

> "Though I walk through the valley of the shadow of death I will fear no evil," he murmured; "for Thou art with me. Thy rod and Thy staff they comfort me."

The twenty-third psalm. Michael remembered how it had always been a favourite with the Gzendis, and now Bembi was repeating it as a prayer of thankfulness.

> "Thou anointest my head with oil. My cup runneth over. Surely goodness and mercy shall follow me all the days of my life, and I will dwell in the House of the Lord for ever. Amen."

Michael finished the psalm. The three looked at one another. Bound as they were, at the mercy of Kikembu and knowing that evil things were being done in the village, they were strengthened in the knowledge that they were not alone, that God was with them.

It's strange, Michael reflected; I had already made up my mind to be a missionary, and I have tried to be a true follower of the Lord, Jesus Christ. Yet I didn't really understand until now what it means to feel Jesus so near to me. Yes, through their trials, these three were learning how the presence of God can strengthen and sustain them.

The incident of the snake and mongoose had, of course, distracted their attention, but great gusts of smoke which eddied past the doorway and the crackling sound of burning timber left no doubt in their minds that Kikembu, with the help of the Gzendis, was carrying out his threat.

Soon the witch-doctor would return to the hut, no doubt expecting to find that the snake had completed his plan. What would he do when he found that they were still there?

The three discussed their plight, but again they could do nothing but wait. Yet the thought of escape still ran through Michael's mind. If only I could get to the hospital. The wish burned in his brain. He knew he could not save the building now, but he remembered the vaccines which his father had only three days ago received from the coast. Should there be an outbreak of fever or small-pox, those vaccines would be without price.

His father had told him with what difficulty he had procured them, and to Michael it was galling to lie there, bound and unable to do anything.

He started as a shadow passed across the doorway. Was this Kikembu's dreaded return?

"Chief Bembi. You there?" The voice in a hoarse whisper startled them all.

"Baluki!" Michael gasped. "Bembi, it's Baluki!"

"Yes, we are here," Bembi replied softly. "We are bound. My children make me prisoner."

The fat figure of Baluki appeared at the doorway, crawling in a ludicrous manner on all fours. He glanced right and left, then entered. Perspiration glistened on his fat face.

"I no come before. I afraid," he stammered. "But I couldn't leave you."

"Unbind us, friend Baluki," Bembi commanded. "Soon it would have been too late."

"Yes, chief Bembi," Baluki stammered. His nerves were on edge. He kept glancing nervously over his shoulder. Somehow, however, his trembling fingers managed to undo the ropes. "I go into jungle," he explained, gabbling away. "I afraid. I see fire. I afraid again. But I come."

"And jolly brave of you it was too," gasped Michael as he tore the last of the rope from his hands. "Bembi and Gezi, run with Baluki into the jungle. Go to that place where we were last night. I'll be with you later."

"Michael, my son, come back——" the old chief cried out.

It was too late.

Michael tore down the beaten mud street. The school and chapel were blazing, great tongues of fire leaping into the air. The main body of the Gzendis and Kikembu were clustered about the hospital. This was a large one-storey building, built of wood, with a corrugated-iron roof. Already smoke was billowing through the seams of the timbers.

The crowd about the hospital did not notice him until he was in their midst. He pushed his way unceremoniously through them, and they were in such a state of hysteria that they took no notice of him. Kikembu had so worked them up by now that they had no realisation of what they were doing. They were like irresponsible children, and the leaping flames of fire had a weird fascination for them.

Kikembu, however, did not miss the figure of the boy as he dashed through the crowd. He kept his power by watching every point. Yet he was not prepared for this. Quite anticipating that his evil plan with the snake was complete, his jaw fell at the sight of Michael, and his eyes held a glint of fear.

The building loomed before Michael. He knew exactly what he had to do. The vaccines were carefully packed in a box. His father had placed the box in his small laboratory as soon as it had arrived. Nevertheless it was a task to daunt anyone. Through the open doorways he could see red streaks of flame and thick, billowing smoke.

He did not hesitate. There was a prayer on his lips for strength as he dashed into the building, his handkerchief tied tightly around his nostrils. The smoke and heat hit him like the blast from a furnace and sent him back. Again he dashed in. A crackling timber fell across his path. He leapt over it.

The beds of the ward were smouldering. The wooden walls were ablaze. His eyes stung as though pricked with a thousand red-hot needles. His clothes were scorched and the heat blistered his body. Still he dashed on through the ward and into the small laboratory at the end.

Michael sighed with relief. The fire had not reached this part. There was the small box. He clutched hold of it. His mind worked fast. There was a small window

43

in the laboratory. It opened out on to a sloping roof at the back of the building. This would be a better escape than through the ward.

With not a moment to waste, he hoisted himself up to the window, hauled himself through and slid down the roof to the ground. How thankful he was to feel the strong, hard earth beneath him! Without a backward glance, he dashed towards the jungle. He hadn't been able to save much, but this box that he carried could be without price should an emergency arise.

It wasn't until he reached the safety of the jungle and had thrown himself down into the tall elephant grass to rest and thank God for his escape, that it occurred to him that the hospital had been empty.

Where were the sick people? Normally at least half of the beds were occupied. And where were Saluki and Tensam, the young Africans who acted as orderlies and nurses in the hospital? They had always been loyal and loved their work. Had Kikembu harmed them too?

Michael felt very worried as he rose from his knees and made his way towards the clearing in the jungle. Now that he had lost touch with the witch-doctor, how would he ever find his father and mother? Yet he could do nothing at present by staying in Filembu.

CHAPTER FIVE

IT wasn't easy for Michael to make his way through the tall elephant grass and the tangled undergrowth of the jungle. He had only a vague idea of the direction to the clearing, for when he had travelled that way before, it had been night.

To add to his discomfiture and his tiredness, the tropical rain now began to fall in earnest, penetrating through the umbrella of the mighty trees so that he was soon wet through and his body smarted painfully from the burns he had received in the hospital fire.

He trudged desperately, but after a few minutes he knew that he was lost. It was a terrible situation. He had, he knew, acted impetuously, but he had had to do things quickly, and his plan had been the first that came to his head.

He sank down wearily. His strength seemed to ebb away and, in a daze, he began to wonder whether this was to be the end, after all. He prayed, but somehow his eyes were so heavy that he couldn't keep them open. The only thing he wanted to do was to sleep. The reaction from his adventures now came upon him with full force.

Yet he knew he must not sleep, must not give in. So much depended on him. Bembi and Gezi and Baluki were waiting for him; and would their faith hold if he

never reached them? And if they failed, what of his
father and mother?

"Hallo—hallo——"

It was only a dream that cry. What did they call it—
an hallucination? He was only imagining it.

"Hallo—hallo——"

The cry was nearer now and clearer. Could it really
be somebody calling?

With a strangled cry from his parched throat, he
called back, "Hallo—hallo——"

No, this couldn't be his imagination. He could hear
the slash of the elephant grass as though a body were
thrusting towards him.

"Hallo—hallo——" he yelled weakly. His throat
felt as if it must burst as he made the effort.

Yes, now he was sure. Somebody was very near. But
was it friend or foe? He felt too tired to worry—just so
long as it was somebody.

"Master Michael!"

He looked up and his heart leapt with joy and relief.
Bending over him was a young man of about twenty, a
green fez on his head and a blue robe about his strong,
lithe body. And the young man's black face was one
broad grin. His brown eyes laughed with pleasure.

"Saluki!" Michael gasped. "Gee! I am glad to see
you."

His father had always said it was a pleasure to have
Saluki about the hospital. He even went as far as to say
that this young hospital assistant's smile was worth a
bottle of medicine to his patients. How completely
Michael agreed with him at that moment!

"Come, take my arm, Master Michael," he said.

46

"Come on. Soon you will jump over the trees. Everything is going to be all right, except for the rain. And that's a change. Up you come. See, my arm is strong."

Michael was too tired to ask questions. All he wanted was to feel that strong arm of Saluki's about him and to be reassured by the gay presence of this young African.

"What a time! Master Michael," Saluki grinned as he half carried him through the jungle. "What a time! That Kikembu is a bad man, but I wasn't afraid of him. I laughed at his silly antics."

Oh, it was good to listen to him. He seemed to make light of all the troubles that had come upon Filembu.

"But when he said he was going to burn down the hospital, then I said to myself that this is more than bad. I must do something." He frowned, and his brown eyes flashed.

"How did you know? I mean, weren't you in the jungle last night?" Michael asked.

"Oh, no." Saluki grinned. "I'm very important. Kikembu came to see me first. He told me what he was going to do. He asked me to help him. He said he would make me a witch-doctor like himself. Ha! ha! Can you imagine me as a witch-doctor?" He contorted his face, and the effect was so comical that Michael, despite his weakness, burst out laughing.

"Oh no, I'm a follower of the Lord Jesus Christ," he went on more seriously. "I love God. He has forgiven my sins and I have a great joy in my heart. Tensam feels the same. No, we promised Kikembu nothing. We just looked at him, but our brains were working quickly. Steady, Master Michael. You mustn't let a

47

blade of grass push you over. Ah yes, Tensam and I were very cunning."

"I don't believe it," Michael protested weakly. "Thanks for helping me. You're not cunning, Saluki; you're just brave and loyal, and my father and mother will be very grateful. I had a job getting the vaccines."

"Ah, yes, the vaccines." Saluki's face took on a woe-begone air. "That was something I forgot. Ah, there was I thinking I was the cleverest fellow in all Filembu, and I forgot the vaccines. But I did save the patients."

"You—did—what?" Michael gasped.

"Tensam and I wrapped up all the patients—six of them—when Kikembu and all the rest were in the jungle. Ah! It was easy, except for Mrs. Sefuli. Oh dear, what a noise that woman made! You know, I think Mrs. Sefuli is the noisiest woman in all the world. She screamed so much that we were sure everybody would hear her." Saluki grinned mischievously. "We put a handkerchief over her mouth. Was that very bad of us?"

"I'm sure you didn't hurt her," Michael laughed.

"Then we carried them all here into the jungle, where it was safe," Saluki went on to explain. "Oh, it was easy, with the stretchers. Except for old Baromba. You know what a big, fat man Baromba is. He was very heavy, and complained that we bumped him. Ah! And he rolled his big eyes. He thought we were going to take him to the leopards."

"You did all that," gasped Michael, "whilst I was doing nothing. Tell me, Saluki, where are they all now?"

"You did plenty." Saluki nodded his head emphatic-
ally. "Bembi told me all about it."

"I don't understand. Have you seen them? Where
are they? I was trying to find them," Michael stammered.

Saluki stopped and lowered him gently to the ground.
"We're nearly there. I took the patients to the clearing
after Kikembu went. Then Bembi, Gezi and Baluki
came. They told me everything. I came to find you,
Master Michael. You were very brave. I take off my
hat to you." He raised his fez and bowed low. Then he
winked. His black face was full of fun. What a grand
fellow Saluki was! "Hippee, up again. We shall soon
be there."

"Just a minute, Saluki." Michael hesitated. This was
the most important question, and he feared the answer.
"My father and mother—did Kikembu say anything
about them?"

Saluki's face fell, and for the first time his boisterous
good humour deserted him. "He said they would
trouble us no more," he replied slowly. "But come,
Master Michael; we will find them as soon as you are
strong. Kikembu will be afraid to harm them too
much."

"Do you really believe that, or are you saying it just
to please me?" Michael insisted.

The young African grinned. "No, I always speak the
truth. Kikembu is really afraid of the white man—the
officials in uniform. But we must find them. We must.
Filembu will not be the same until Kikembu goes."

"Thanks." Michael sighed. He felt in his pocket and
drew out the little mongoose. The tiny fellow glanced

up cheekily with his sharp, bright eyes. "Look, Saluki, this was a present from Gezi. Isn't he a fine fellow? I'd forgotten he was still there. He might have got hurt, but he's all right, isn't he?"

"Ah, yes, the mongoose is a mighty fine fellow," Saluki laughed. "He's brave and he laughs and he's a very good friend."

"Just like you," Michael murmured to himself. Yes, there was quite a likeness between the mongoose who now snuggled into his pocket again and this happy, laughing African.

Soon they reached the clearing. There were Michael's friends and the patients, sitting comfortably under an awning supported by bamboo poles which protected them from the rain. A fire blazed, and over it, hanging from a tripod, was a large pot. The appetising smell which floated across reminded Michael that he was ravenously hungry.

Bembi, Gezi and Baluki scrambled to their feet. "Isser!" they called in greeting and relief. Baluki, Michael noticed, was now his fat, jovial self again, and almost as soon as he had welcomed Michael he sat down on the ground again to finish with noisy smacking of his lips a large bowl of steaming stew. "Me hungry," he grunted, and his black face was one wide grin.

Bembi, the old chief, was more moved. Dignified and upright, despite his age, he walked slowly towards Michael and placed his arms on the boy's shoulders.

"Michael, my son," he said slowly. "You are safe. Now I will thank God who has brought you out of the valley of the shadow of death."

And Gezi grasped his hand and smiled quietly. "I, too, will thank God," he whispered.

After a good meal from the steaming pot, Michael felt refreshed and almost recovered from his adventures. Saluki attended to his burns, and then Michael looked round at the six patients whom Saluki and Tensam had made comfortable on blankets. Whatever misgivings Mrs. Sefuli may have had about her sudden upheaval from the hospital, she now seemed quite content, and as for Baromba, he was sitting up, looking little the worse for his adventure.

It was all very rough-and-ready, however. This state of affairs couldn't go on. These sick people needed his father's skilful attention. If they remained long in this condition there might be serious consequences. Not that, he knew, Saluki and Tensam could have done more.

He studied Tensam more carefully. This African was a little older than Saluki, thin, tall and rather solemn-faced. There was a gentle firmness about him that made you trust him immediately. He was the one who now passed from one patient to another, speaking quietly to them and encouraging them.

With only a brief, shy smile, he had greeted Michael, and then gone about his tasks. Michael remembered how his father had often said that Tensam was a born doctor, that one day he should go to college and be properly trained.

Well, there they were, almost like outcasts, in the clearing of the jungle with the equatorial rain beating down upon their rough covering, with little food and with the knowledge that Kikembu, the witch-doctor, was in undisputed charge of Filembu. What were they to do?

They talked about it for a long time. One thing became clear. The only persons who could fight against Kikembu's power over the Gzendis were Michael's father and mother. Bembi could no nothing. He was, in fact, under the curse of death. The appearance of the missionaries against them—especially after Kikembu telling them that their power had been broken—might turn the scales. Yes, the finding of the missionaries was their only hope. But how were they to do it?

Bembi was the wise counsellor in this. They must, he said, go to Goez. It would be a hazardous adventure. But go somebody must.

He had a friend there, he told them—Effendi—and he would help. If anybody knew what was happening, it would be Effendi.

Now followed a heated argument as to who should set out on this perilous adventure. Bembi and Gezi were all for going alone. Baluki did not insist, pleading that his fat bulk would be more of an hindrance than a help. Tensam quietly insisted that he should go. But Saluki won the day. Who better to go than he and Michael, he grinned? They were young and Tensam must stop behind to care for the sick.

So it was settled. A small portion of the rations which Saluki had rescued when hurriedly vacating the hospital were portioned out to the two adventurers and all was ready except for the most important thing.

The party of fugitives from Filembu knelt down to pray. They committed Saluki and Michael to God on their journey, asking for strength and guidance. They thanked God for their deliverance up to the present time, and for the first time they remembered the Gzendis in their prayers, asking God to bring them back into the paths of truth and goodness. Then there was a special prayer for Michael's father and mother, for each carried a lingering doubt in his mind that something terrible might have happened to them.

Thus, fortified in God's strength, Saluki and Michael set out for Goez.

CHAPTER SIX

SALUKI knew the trail that led to Goez, and he trod along confidently. Above, in the great, towering trees, the monkeys skuttled from branch to branch, chattering endlessly. There was the scurry of wild animals, scared by their approach. A dank smell came from the undergrowth. And all the time the torrential rain beat through, so that it was like walking through a warm shower.

Saluki was in the highest of spirits. To comfort Michael, he may have acted more confidently than he really felt, but he kept up a constant patter of lively talk, and once he burst out in great gusts of laughter.

"Fancy me being assistant to Kikembu, the witch-doctor," he roared. "Can you imagine me stewing things up in a pot and making magic spells?"

Michael laughed with him. Saluki belonged to the new race of Africans. He had been trained in the Mission school. He was a Christian. He had not the fears of such men as Baluki and Gezi, and even Bembi.

"Wonder why he came to you first?" Michael asked him.

"He thought, no doubt, that I knew all the secrets of the white man's magic, as he calls it," Saluki grinned. "He imagines that medicine is magic, you know. And as I was helping in the hospital, he thought I could let him into the mysteries. But—yee-hee—I wouldn't."

Michael needed all Saluki's help during that arduous journey. He still felt the effects of his adventures. They followed a hunter's trail, barely eighteen inches wide. There were giant trees, but sometimes they came to wide swamps with reeds and bamboos, and there they had to plunge knee-deep into the thick, slimy mud. Then there were the expanses of bush and grasses, sometimes six feet tall, in which trailing plants made the going almost impossible. Only by swift, deft strokes of his bush-knife did Saluki manage to carve a way for them.

Pheasants of a brilliant blue colour flew about the trees, and now and again Saluki drew Michael's attention to the beat of the crested eagle's wings which made the monkeys crouch in terror. Hundreds of brilliantly coloured butterflies fluttered before them.

It was a new world to Michael—a journey that, in Saluki's company, he would have been fascinated by were it not for the danger that hung over them.

How thankful Michael was to reach the streams which ran through the jungle and there to feel the cool water upon his aching limbs !

They were four hours making their journey to Goez, and by the end of it Michael was ready to drop with fatigue. Saluki placed his strong arm under Michael's arms and helped him along the last hundred yards until they reached the edge of the clearing in which the native village of Goez nestled. There they flung themselves down into the tall grass to discuss plans.

This village was little different from Filembu. There were the mud huts with their queer, conical-shaped roofs of thatched palm leaves. The palaver house stood a little aloof from the village. The rice-fields came right up to the edge of the jungle. It had stopped raining now, and the villagers were busy in the fields, most of them wearing white robes, and some with an assortment of straw hats, trilby and bowler hats on their heads.

It seemed peaceful enough, as though nothing had ever happened. Yet Michael and Saluki knew it was to this place that the missionaries had been summoned for help and that here Kikembu had laid his evil plans.

"We have to find Effendi first," Saluki said thoughtfully. "But how? I do not know the people of Goez, and if they have been up to mischief they will not welcome us."

"I'm sure father and mother are there," Michael exclaimed. "We've got to find out, Saluki."

"We will wait until nightfall," the young African said. "We must act cautiously, and it will give you time to rest, too."

So they lay in the long grass hidden from view of the village, their only food the rice that Saluki carried in a small pouch hanging from his waist. And Michael slept.

He was awakened by a gentle shaking. "Come," Saluki whispered. "It is time to go down to the village."

They knelt for a few minutes, committing themselves to God, and then set out.

In the blackness of the African night, with but the flickering lights from the window-openings of the huts to guide them, Goez seemed suddenly to have an atmosphere of danger. Silently they crept up upon it. There was no formulated plan in their minds. They had

56

decided to snatch any opportunity that was offered them.

They passed by the first huts. Listening outside, they could hear the subdued murmur of conversation and the whimper of a child asleep. Down the street, which after the heavy rain was like a morass, they plodded, bending low and not daring to speak to one another. A faint stirring at the doorway of one of the huts and the appearance of a heavily-built man silhouetted against the soft glow of the wood-fire made them throw themselves to the ground.

They lay there for several seconds in the slimy mud before they felt it safe to rise again. It all seemed so hopeless. What *could* they do? They stood, listening hard and completely at a loss. Then they began to plod down the street again, making towards the palaver house.

"Isser!" The familiar greeting of the Gzendis came to them in a soft whisper.

They turned quickly. The heavily-built man stood in the doorway again, and he beckoned to them urgently. They ran towards him, and he pushed them unceremoniously into his hut.

In the dim light they could see that he was a giant of a man, and the firelight flickered over the great muscles of his black chest, which was bare. He wore a pair of khaki shorts.

"You are the missionary's son," he grunted. His black, shining face betrayed no emotion. "And you— who are you?"

"I am Saluki, assistant at the hospital at Filembu——"

57

"Ah! I am Effendi. I watch for you all day. I see you come. Very foolish. Others might have seen. I keep watch for you."

"Do you mean you actually *saw* us when we were in the jungle?" Michael gasped.

Effendi nodded, but did not smile. "I keep watch these three days. I expect someone. Bad business in Goez. Very bad business."

"Bembi told us that you would be our friend," said Michael urgently. "Do you know what has happened to my father and mother?"

Effendi folded his great arms across his chest and frowned. "They are well—at the moment. But there is danger. Listen, I tell you."

He indicated mats around the wood-fire, and the three sat down.

"When the missionaries came to Filembu they teach us many things. They teach us about God who sent His Son, Jesus, into the world to die for us," Effendi began. "That was good news for the Gzendis, and many of us became Christians. That was good too. But some hated the missionaries and the white man and God."

"You mean Kikembu?" Michael interjected.

Effendi nodded his head solemnly. "There were others too, but mostly Kikembu. They went into the bush and wait their time. Now they come back and they say, 'No white man in Africa'. They say, 'We go back to the old gods'."

"I see," Saluki said, and his face was unusually solemn. "Look here, Michael; this is even bigger than we thought. If Kikembu is the leader of one of the groups to drive out the white man from Africa, we're

58

up against a bigger thing even than we thought. You see, this sort of thing is happening all over Africa."

"Then he's more than a witch-doctor?" Michael asked in surprise.

"I'm afraid so. Or, at least, that's what it sounds like," Saluki explained. "Of course, he's using his witchcraft to impress the Africans. That would be part of his plan. But if there are others who think as he does in the area, then there must be trouble brewing."

"You speak right," Effendi grunted. "Three men come with Kikembu from the bush. They now at palaver house. They have your father and mother prisoner."

"Then—they're not dead!" Michael gasped in relief. "Oh, this is good news. What can we do, Effendi?"

The massive African shrugged. "That I do not know. People in Goez good people, but Kikembu come and make them afraid. They give food to Kikembu's friends and for your father and mother, but they do not interfere. Kikembu wait until he safe and then——"

Michael shuddered. Effendi, merely by a shrug, had shown how dangerous was the position of the missionaries.

"Look here, Saluki," Michael urged. "We've got to do something."

Effendi held up his hand. "First," he said, "you tell me what has happened at Filembu."

Quickly Michael and Saluki told their story. Effendi sat, listening intently and occasionally grunting, but still the expression on his face was stern, giving no indication of his feelings.

"Then there are Bembi and Gezi, you two and this

Tensam," he muttered. "Baluki I know, and he not very much good. It is perhaps enough."

"Enough for what?" Saluki asked.

"To make stand against Kikembu," Effendi grunted. "Up to now I only one in Goez. I good Christian. I love God, but alone I can do nothing. Now, with the others of you, I feel strong. Tonight we go to palaver house." He stood upright, a giant of a man, and for the first time he smiled. "The missionaries shall teach again, and everybody learn to love God. When they are free, they know what to do."

Saluki and Michael looked at one another with relief. Effendi had expressed in his own way what their thoughts had been, and there was no doubt the strength of purpose of this muscular African.

"Tonight," Effendi continued, "Kikembu's friends sleep well. They drink a lot. They think they're safe because everybody afraid of Kikembu. Come! We go!"

They followed close behind the African as he led them through the village to the palaver house. He placed his finger to his lips, warning them to silence, when they came to the large, open-sided building.

Now they could hear the sound of heavy breathing, and knew that Effendi's forecast was true. Like a swift, black shadow, Effendi slid silently into the palaver house. Michael and Saluki stood outside, holding their breath. They heard a grunt as one of the captors turned in his sleep. Then a scuffle. Unable to restrain himself, Michael crept up close to the wall and peered in.

He could just make out the figures of three dark men, stretched out on mats on the floor. But the back of the palaver house was inky-black—and still. Whatever Effendi might be doing, he worked silently.

It seemed to Michael that he stared into the inky darkness for hours. Then he heard the slight scrape of a shoe on the hard floor. Effendi's great form loomed into sight. Behind him came two other figures.

Michael's heart was in his mouth. It was almost more than he could do to repress the yell of relief that came into his throat. Effendi clapped his great hand over Michael's mouth.

"Quiet!" he hissed.

The four crept silently behind Effendi down the mud street, passing the villagers' huts. Every moment they expected somebody to come out and give the alarm, but at last they reached Effendi's hut and sighed their relief.

"Oh, Mum and Dad, are you all right?" gasped Michael, and hugged his mother.

His father, a medium-built man, thin faced, with bright, piercing eyes, clapped him on the shoulder.

"Well, Michael," he smiled. "It *is* good to see you. Your mother and I were beginning to wonder what was going to happen to us. But Effendi, our good friend here, has rescued us, and we're together once again."

"How are you, Mother?" Michael was so excited that the words almost choked in his throat. "Did they treat you badly? Have they hurt you? Have——"

Mrs. Jameson, a small woman with a pleasant face and yet a determined air about her, laughed at his eagerness.

"No, Michael," she replied gently. "Not nearly so badly as you might think. Of course, they bound us up

c   61

and kept us in the palaver house. But they didn't hurt us, and fed us well. Now we are anxious to know what it is all about.''

"Yes," Mr. Jameson interposed. "We had that call to Goez because there were supposed to be some cases of fever here. Then, as soon as we arrived, we were tied up and put in the palaver house. That's all we know. What has been happening? We've been worried out of our lives.''

Rapidly Michael recounted all that had been happening at Filembu and how he and Saluki had come to Goez to search for them. As he unfolded the story, Mr. Jameson's face because anxious and worried.

"And now you say the school and the hospital and the chapel are burned down," he said gravely. "Why, things couldn't be more serious. It seems to me that it is all a very deeply laid plain.''

"Michael rescued the vaccines," Saluki smiled, announcing his presence.

"Oh, Saluki." Mr. Jameson pressed the young African's hand. "Thanks for all you've done. The patients are, I believe, in the clearing. Good work! You and Tensam have been good friends—and Michael, you've been a brick too.'' He turned to the giant African, Effendi, who stood a little aloof. "Thanks to you, Effendi, also. What trouble you have got yourself into this night I do not know, but we are grateful.''

Effendi did not smile. "I do things sooner," he grunted. "But I alone in Goez. I could do nothing alone.''

"Yes." Mr. Jameson nodded his head. "I understand that. Now, before we decide what we are going

do, I think we'd better sum up the position. Kikembu
evidently a leader of some terrorist group as well as a
itch-doctor. The drought gave him his opportunity. He
atices us to Goez and then plays his tricks at Filembu
ntil he has them in his power. That accomplished, I
ppose he would have come back to Goez and——"
e spread his hands expressively. "But, thank God,
ou arrived in time."

"I've just thought, Dad," Michael burst in. "Your
aki shirt, he sent it to the Mission house all blood-
ained. I thought——"

"Another trick, I'm afraid," his father interrupted.
No, he did not dare to harm us—then."

"You go quick from Goez," Effendi grunted. "Here
is not safe. If they wake and find you gone, all village
after us."

Mr. Jameson's brow puckered into a frown. He had
ken charge of the situation, and there was an air of
thority about him. Michael was glad to hand over
e responsibility for he knew that things were now be-
nd him.

"Yes, Effendi," he replied. "We must go. Here we
n do little. Kikembu is the centre of the trouble, and
have got to face him. And you, Effendi, you must
me with us. Here your life will not be worth a scrap
paper when they discover what has happened. They
ll know it was you."

"I not afraid." Effendi gave a half-smile. "I have
od with me. He will look after me."

"Yes," Mr. Jameson replied. "I know and I under-
nd, Effendi. You have kept strong in the faith, but
must keep together now—all of us who are not

afraid of Kikembu. And I shall need your help, Effend
Please come.''

Gravely the African nodded, and then he reall
smiled. "I come," he grunted.

"I shall go to Filembu," the missionary said. "Ho
about you, Sarah? Do you feel up to it?"

Mrs. Jameson nodded her head and smiled bravel
"I'm ready," she said.

"And before we start," Mr. Jameson said quietl
"we must ask God's guidance."

What lay before them, they were none of them sur
At Filembu there was danger. At Goez there w
danger. Yet God had preserved them, and they truste
in Him to guide them. They offered their thanks
Him, and then Mr. Jameson mentioned Kikembu
his prayer, asking that the witch-doctor might be l
into the way of salvation.

That puzzled Michael. After all that Kikembu ha
done, it hardly seemed likely that he would chan
his evil ways. He determined to talk to his father abo
it later, but in the meantime he was full of relief th
his father and mother were safe.

CHAPTER SEVEN

IT was with a certain amount of misgiving that the party left Goez in the dead of the night. They felt somehow that they were deserting the villagers. Yet, as Mr. Jameson pointed out, the trouble was centred in Kikembu, and he must be met before the evil spread. How they were to deal with the witch-doctor was a matter they had to leave until the moment of meeting, and in that they felt sure of God's guidance.

They reached the jungle without mishap. After the heavy rains, the night was bright with stars, twinkling from a dark, mauve sky, and for that they were thankful.

Saluki now took charge of the route back. Humming gaily to himself, and his black face one large smile, he led once again through the jungle, but this time he followed a different track, one which led through even deeper jungle, but which, he told them, would bring them in a short time to the banks of a river where they could rest until sunrise.

It took them an hour to reach this spot, and gladly they threw themselves down on the river-bank. Effendi could not, however, rest. He stood a little way off from the four, his dark face impassive, his arms folded across his massive chest. He would, he said, keep guard.

Yet Michael could not sleep. The relief of finding his

father and mother was too great. He crept up close to his father, who sat staring thoughtfully into the black shining water of the river. His mother and Saluki were stretched out in the thick grass, asleep.

"What's the matter, Son?" Mr. Jameson asked. "Can't you rest?" He put his arm round Michael's shoulders.

"No, I've been thinking about it all, Dad. There's so much I want to know. You prayed for Kikembu, and I wondered why you did that. Oh, Dad, how is it all going to end? What's going to happen to us?"

Mr. Jameson patted his shoulder. "I know; it's all very puzzling, isn't it?" he said. "You are fourteen now, Michael, and, with God's help, you're going to be a missionary. Perhaps the time has arrived when we ought to have a long chat about things, eh?"

Michael looked up eagerly into his father's face. "Please, Dad," he begged.

"It'll take a little time, Son," Mr. Jameson began, "because we've got to go back to the beginning of time to understand the situation in which we find ourselves and why now I am praying earnestly in my heart for Kikembu."

Behind them was the black jungle. It was quiet now except for the croaking of frogs down by the river. Michael lay back to listen to the quiet voice of his father.

"You see, God made men and women to be happy and to live in His love, surrounded by all the beautiful things He had created. It is a very lovely world, you know, Michael; and if only men and women had loved Him in return and had not been selfish and sinful, giv-

66

ing way to temptations, then we could have enjoyed God's presence. But things did go wrong."

"You mean the story in Genesis?" Michael asked.

His father nodded. "Yes, it is very clear there, isn't it? Men disobeyed God and wanted their own way, and so they sinned, for sinning is just disobedience to God's commands and wishes."

"And, you know, all the time we are sinning, we can't be right with God, can we? Do you remember when you were seven how cross I was with you?"

"Don't I just!" Michael smiled. "I got in a temper about something and threw Mum's best tea-pot on to the floor. Seems funny sitting here and talking about that now, Dad."

"Yes, perhaps it does; but it's all tied up," his father went on. "You see, for a time we weren't right with one another. I was cross and you had your temper. And it wasn't put right until you had said you were sorry and I forgave you. Yet it didn't finish there, did it?"

"No, I remember." Now Michael laughed. "You said I'd have to pay for the broken tea-pot out of my pocket-money. Gee! I did have a struggle."

"But you never paid in full for that tea-pot," his father smiled. "Your mother—she told me afterwards —put a shilling every week to your twopence. Why, you never could have paid for the tea-pot yourself. The price was too great."

"Did she really do that?" Michael gasped.

His father nodded. "Now, God doesn't get cross with us when we do wrong, but He is greatly hurt because He loves us so much and He knows we cannot pay the price of our sin. It is far too great. That's why

He sent His Son, Jesus Christ, into the world. He had never sinned, and when He died on the Cross He died for all our sins. He paid the whole price. Do you remember the hymn, 'There was none other good enough to pay the price of sin'? So that, if we are really sorry about the wrong things we have done and are determined to try never to do them again, then God can forgive us and we shall be right—reconciled is the word—with Him. It's as simple—and as lovely—as that."

"Yes." Michael pondered. "I've always understood it something like that. But where does Kikembu come in?"

"Ah!" Mr. Jameson contemplated the bright stars in the sky for a few moments. "When Jesus came to Palestine. He told them of the love of God. Many listened and believed. But there were others who hated Him. And these worked on the fears and superstitions of the ordinary people so that in the end they cried, 'Crucify Him!'—even those who before had believed."

"I see," Michael exclaimed. "Just like Kikembu worked on the Gzendis and made them burn down the chapel and everything."

"Yes," his father said. "Kikembu is an evil man who does not like the things that Jesus taught because he is selfish and wants power for himself. When Jesus was dying on the Cross, He cried, 'Father, forgive them, for they know not what they do.' You see, He was dying for the sins of us all, even for those who put Him to death, and He prayed that God would forgive them."

"And Kikembu?" The question half-formed on Michael's lips.

"Yes," Mr. Jameson said. "Jesus died for the sins of Kikembu, even though he is evil and, like the priests of old, has led good people into doing evil things. Even now I can hear Jesus saying, 'Forgive Kikembu because he doesn't know what he is doing.'

"We've got to try and tell him that. We've to try to make him repent for all his evil, and we must teach him about the love of God, and how he may be saved from his sins because Jesus died on a cross for him."

"I understand, Dad," Michael whispered.

"That's why we must go back to Filembu," Mr. Jameson said. "Oh, yes, there would be an easier way. We could make tracks to the nearest police patrol and report all that has happened. We may have to do later, of course. But that is not the way of Christ. We must first give Kikembu the chance of finding salvation. So there it is, Michael. Now I think you ought to try and sleep. And, Michael, now we're alone, I'm proud of you and all the things you've done. It was splendid of you to rescue the vaccines."

Michael curled himself up on the ground. All that his father had told him sank into his mind. In all the dangerous excitement, he had been unable to see things clearly. Now that his father had explained, he could understand, and as he lay there his prayer was for Kikembu and that he might be led into the way of salvation.

The party were astir as soon as dawn broke, and they prepared to leave. It was not until that moment that they missed Effendi. They were thrown into a state of consternation.

"Do you remember, Michael," Mr. Jameson said

with a worried frown. "He *was* standing up there by the trees when we were chatting, wasn't he?"

"Yes, Dad," Michael agreed. "I remember as well as anything because he looked so strong and tall."

"No harm could have come to him, surely," Mr. Jameson rubbed his chin. "It's strange, though. Effendi wouldn't go off just like that."

"You don't think that the men from Goez——" Mrs. Jameson began to voice the fears of them all.

"I shouldn't think so," Mr. Jameson said doubtfully. "But we've got to be prepared for anything. Look, we've got to make a search."

"I'll go." Saluki stepped forward eagerly. "You must stay here with Mrs. Jameson. In the jungle you'd get lost. Let me take Michael with me."

The missionary frowned. "I don't like it, Saluki," he confessed. "It means splitting up the party, but we must do all we can to find Effendi. Yes, go. It is better for two than one, and may God go with you."

Thus Michael found himself alone in the jungle once again with Saluki, but now they followed no known track. Effendi might be anywhere. For a time Saluki's good-humoured chatter deserted him and his face bore a look of intense concentration. For half an hour they made a circuit of fifty yards from the river bank. Then Saluki shrugged.

"Let's go back again," he said. "You must point out to me exactly where you saw Effendi last night."

They examined the spot carefully. Saluki went down on his knees. Trained to jungle life, and with the inborn instinct of the native, he jumped up suddenly. "Footprints. Yippee! These must be Effendi's."

Michael knelt down in the short grass where Saluki was pointing. The ground was damp, and now that he looked closely there were slight indentations that, without Saluki's keen sight, would have been missed.

Saluki stood there, pondering for a few moments, and then began to follow the trail which would be invisible to anybody who was not trained in jungle lore.

"H'm!" He muttered "Effendi was alone. There are no others tracks but his. Yet it is strange. He walks as though he were limping. See, one foot drags."

No matter how carefully he examined the ground, Michael could not discern all this. He could only glance at Saluki in wondering admiration.

"Come on," Saluki urged. "We must follow the trail. It's all very puzzling."

Michael was content to walk behind the young African and leave it all to him. They soon left the banks of the river and plunged deep into the jungle. Now the trail became clear even to Michael. The tall grass was swathed aside as though a body had stumbled a way through.

Saluki grunted several times. "Effendi was in trouble," he muttered. "What could have been the matter with him? Still there is only one track."

For an hour they pushed through the undergrowth, skirting the trunks of giant trees. Then they came to the bush and Saluki slashed away with his bush-knife. Suddenly he gave an exclamation of dismay and pointed.

"Just over there! It must be Effendi! But he lies still. Quickly, Michael!"

They found the great African where he had

71

collapsed, half supported by the sharp branches of the bush.

"Effendi!" Saluki shook him gently. "What is the matter? What has happened to you?"

Slowly Effendi opened his eyes.

"Go away," he panted. Beads of perspiration glistened on his black face. "Go away. No use. Effendi die."

"Tell us quickly what has happened," Saluki urged. "We're not leaving you."

He placed his arm beneath the massive shoulders and eased Effendi up.

The African's breathing came in short gasps. His brown eyes rolled.

"Snake-bite." He panted. "In the leg. Foolish to let snake bite." He fell back exhausted. "You all go to Filembu. Leave Effendi to die. He happy with his God."

Saluki straightened up.

"Look here, Michael, this is serious," he said with a frown. "Effendi's in a bad way. You can see what has happened, can't you? A snake-bite is nearly always fatal. And Effendi dragged himself out here, not expecting us to find him. He didn't want to hold us up."

"Go—to—Filembu—save—the—Gzendis—Effendi not important——" The African made one last effort and then collapsed.

"Poor old Effendi!" Michael exclaimed. "What a brave chap! He was giving his life up so that he wouldn't be in the way. Gee! It's about the most unselfish thing I've ever heard of."

Saluki nodded and smiled. "Not quite, Michael," he

72

reminded him. "Have you forgotten that the Lord Jesus Christ did just that for us? But there's a chance, and we're going to take it. Effendi's strong. If the poison has not gone all over his body, then I can perhaps do something. Look, can you get back to Mr. Jameson straight away and bring him here? He'll know what to do. Meanwhile, I'm going to try something. Off you go, Michael. You've got to make it for Effendi's sake."

The tone of his voice urged Michael on. This was a different side to the young African's nature that he had discovered—a calm, unhurried way of dealing with an emergency. It dispelled all panic from Michael's mind and inspired him on his journey back to his father.

The way that they had beaten through the jungle and bush was clear and Michael dashed along it. He could hear the soft brush of marauding animals against the trees and in the undergrowth, but his task was so urgent that he was unafraid.

He reached his father and mother, breathless. In short, panting sentences, he gave the news.

"Effendi's a brave man," Mr. Jameson observed. "He knows how urgent it is for us to go to Filembu, and he did this. I only hope that we can save him. Lucky I've still got my bag of instruments with me. They didn't take it from me because they thought it was some special magic. Michael, you stop here with your mother and look after her. I'll dash to Effendi and Saluki. The way should be pretty clear, from what you tell me."

"Can't I——" Michael began.

His father was already on his way. "No, Michael,

73

you must stay. We can't leave your mother alone——''

Michael sat down on the river-bank by Mrs. Jameson. "I do hope Effendi's going to be all right," he murmured.

His mother patted his hand. "Your father will do everything he can," she assured him.

"Saluki said a strange thing, Mum," Michael mused. "When I said that Effendi was giving up his life for our sakes, he said, 'Jesus did the same'. It's wonderful, isn't it, that they should have learned these things?"

His mother smiled reminiscently. "That's why your father and I became missionaries—to tell the good news of Jesus. Although, with Kikembu's efforts, it does seem that a lot of our work is being undone."

"I had a long chat with Dad last night when you were asleep. He made it so clear to me."

Michael and his mother sat chatting, waiting for news of Effendi. They prayed, too, kneeling close to one another, and asking for God's help and guidance.

They waited a long time. It was well past midday before the missionary and Saluki returned, bearing between them the great body of Effendi. Mrs. Jameson had prepared a meal of rice from the small ration that Saluki had brought. But in their anxiety all this was forgotten.

Mr. Jameson and Saluki set the body gently down on the grass.

"He's going to be all right," the missionary said quietly. "We were only just in time. Saluki, here, sucked out some of the poison, and now with the injections I have given him and his amazing strength, he should pull through."

"Thank God!" murmured Mrs. Jameson.

"Yes, thanks are indeed due to God," her husband added. "But we cannot move Effendi for two or three days, and I must stay with him. It presents a problem. We've no food. The others are in the clearing in the jungle. And Kikembu is having all his own way in Filembu. We need God's guidance at this moment more than we have ever needed it. I am worried, because the longer Kikembu is in Filembu, the more difficult our task is going to be."

They knelt down, the four of them, and prayed. Effendi lay still on the grass, his breathing heavy but regular. When they got to their feet again, they were strengthened. They did not know how, but each one had the faith in his heart that they would have the way opened up for them.

CHAPTER EIGHT

FOR three days they had to wait in that spot by the river whilst, after twelve hours of delirium, Effendi gradually recovered his strength and declared himself fit to travel. It was an anxious time.

Saluki managed to contrive some sort of shelter by plaiting palm leaves to form a roof. It was crude, but it did keep off the torrential bouts of rain. As for food, they had to depend on fruits and berries, which grew in abundance in the jungle. This kept their hunger at bay, but it was barely satisfying. They were fortunate in one respect—water was close at hand.

And all the time they worried about conditions at Filembu. They talked over the matter for hours, but still could arrive at no settled plan.

"We must leave it in the hands of God," was Mr. Jameson's final verdict.

However, on the fourth day, with a grim smile, Effendi declared that he was ready to go. He looked thinner and shaken, but he was insistent. So the party set off for the clearing, wondering what lay before them.

Their travel through the jungle and bush was slow, for they were weak, but Saluki, in his inimicable way, kept up a chatter of conversation and seemed to find something humorous to say at every step. In fact, Michael's only memory of that journey was the huge smile on Saluki's black face.

The mongoose had by now taken up a permanent abode in Michael's pocket, and slipped only occasionally out to forage for food.

At last they came to the clearing. As soon as he saw them, Bembi strode forward, a look of joy and relief on his old, wizened face.

"We thought, Mr. Jameson," he choked, "that you were all dead. Every day we pray to God. Now, thanks to Him, you are safe. Isser!"

The old chief hugged them all in turn, so great was his emotion. Gezi, in his quiet way, too, was overjoyed, and Baluki, looking perhaps a little thinner—although there was still a lot of him—beamed.

There was little news to tell. Tensam, still quiet and reserved, reported that his patients were well, except Mrs. Sefuli, who, he observed with a mischievous smile, would always complain anyway. Food was their urgent problem. Nearly all they had taken from Filembu had gone.

As for Kikembu, no news had reached them. This they looked upon as strange, because they had been in fear that a search-party would have been sent after them.

But now that Mr. and Mrs. Jameson were safe and with them, everything would be all right. Of that they were sure.

It came as a shock to them when, after the travellers had been forced by Bembi to eat a meal of rice from their scanty stores, Mr. Jameson announced that he must proceed at once to Filembu—alone.

Protests followed this. All knew the dangers, but, as Mr. Jameson pointed out, their position at the moment was perilous, and would get more so as time passed on. In any case, he must face Kikembu.

Saluki pointed out reasonably that he knew the way back, and therefore must go with Mr. Jameson. His offer the missionary accepted reluctantly but when Michael put forward a plea, his father was adamant.

Bembi put in a word at this point unexpectedly.

"Mr. Jameson," he declared, "I know not what lies before. I know not what Kikembu has done to my children, but this, your son Michael, he brave boy. My people know he brave. Maybe he help."

Mr. Jameson pondered on this for several minutes, and then he nodded his head slowly.

"I don't like it," he admitted, "but you have defied Kikembu, and there is something in what Bembi says. All right, you shall come with Saluki; but do, please, be guided by me."

Mrs. Jameson was near to collapse, but she smiled bravely as the three departed.

"May God keep you safe," she whispered.

Saluki led once again through the jungle, but now he said not a word. The peril before them loomed large in their thoughts. They did not feel like talking. Before they left the shelter of the jungle, Mr. Jameson asked them to kneel and pray that God would be with them in their venture and that He would guide them in teaching the witch-doctor the way of salvation.

The village was strangely quiet as they surveyed it from the cover of the trees. The weather was dull, overcast and the air held a damp, sultry heat. Yet it was not raining, and the Gzendis should have been working in the rice-fields. Not one was in sight.

They could see the blackened timbers of the Mission buildings. Mr. Jameson's face fell as he saw that they had been burnt out beyond repair. His bright eyes were misty, and for the first time he hesitated.

"How terrible that they should have done this!" he whispered. "How terrible!"

"We shall rebuild it all, Mr. Jameson," smiled Saluki. "I never did like the old hospital. We'll have a bigger and better one. I shall like that."

"Thanks." The missionary patted his arm. "I'm glad you're with me, if only for that."

"We must be careful," the African lad warned. "I do not like this at all. See, there is nobody in the fields, nobody in the street. It seems that the village is deserted. But how can that be? Mr. Jameson, I fear that some terrible evil has fallen upon Filembu. Look the smoke from the wood-fires comes from the roofs of the huts." He shook his head. "No, I do not like this."

"We must go and see," Mr. Jameson declared, and they made towards the village.

Nobody challenged them as they approached. It was, as Saluki had said, as though the village were deserted, yet the Gzendis were there—either in their huts or engaged on some evil plan with Kikembu.

They passed the Mission house. There was no movement there. Even Mensa seemed to have disappeared. The mud street between the huts was empty, and now they could see the charred remains of the Mission buildings a little farther on. Still there was no movement in Filembu.

"A trap, Mr. Jameson," whispered Saluki. "I fear it is a trap. Come, let us——"

Whatever he was going to say was too late, for there was a sudden patter of feet and the Gzendis poured out of their mud huts and surrounded them.

"Gee! An ambush!" gasped Michael.

Mr. Jameson put his arm round his shoulders. "Do not move," he whispered.

The Gzendis stood in groups around them, yet did not seem to dare to move too close. On their black faces was an expression that Michael had not seen before—a sort of bewildered, frightened look. Gone were the fanatical grimaces that Kikembu had invoked.

"Bembarli." Mr. Jameson addressed a short, tubby man, wearing a black trilby hat and a blue robe. "What has been happening in Filembu? I go away for a few days, and when I come back I find the school, the hospital and the chapel burnt, and I know how this has happened. But, tell me why Filembu is as quiet as a cat that sleeps in the sun, and where is Kikembu, who has led you into evil ways?"

Bembarli shuffled his bare feet in the mud. He looked round despairingly at the other Africans, trying to gain some support. But no one stepped forward or said a word.

"Come, Bembarli," the missionary urged. "In Bembi's absence you are the man in charge. Do not be afraid. I am waiting."

The African gave a great sigh and with a tremendous effort began to speak.

"We have been foolish, Mr. Jameson," he said. "We have been mad. All the Gzendis mad. We listen to Kikembu."

There were murmurs from the crowd. All began to nod their heads in agreement.

"But the madness gone, Mr. Jameson," Bembarli was now trembling, and his brown eyes glanced fearfully in all directions. "We sorry, Mr. Jameson. We have deep sorrow. Do not hurt us, Mr. Jameson. We promise we never do it again."

Despite the terrible things that had happened in Filembu, Mr. Jameson had to smile gently at the African who was so obviously frightened.

"I have not come to harm you, Bembarli," he said. "I have taught you for many years of the God of love, and if you are truly sorry for what you have done then, He will forgive you, and I must too. But tell me, why have you changed, and where is this evil man, Kikembu?"

There were murmurs and groans from the crowd of Gzendis.

"Kikembu sick. He die. Yesterday he take great sickness. He curse Filembu with his sickness. We all die." Bembarli's voice was shrill with fear.

"Tell me where he is," Mr. Jameson said quickly.

"What do you think has happened?" Michael whispered.

"I don't know yet, but I've got a shrewd idea. Now, Bembarli, take me to Kikembu."

The African shook his head uneasily. "No, Mr. Jameson, I'm afraid. You go. He in palaver house. He die——"

"Come on," Mr. Jameson said. "I will talk to these people later. Meanwhile we must see that is wrong with Kikembu."

81

Michael and Saluki followed him as he hurried towards the palaver house. The Gzendis, however, hung back, advancing only a few paces and then retreating. Whatever had happened in the palaver house had given them a mortal terror.

At the entrance to this open-sided building, with its thatched roof of palm leaves, Mr. Jameson turned.

"I want you both to stay outside," he said. "I'd rather face Kikembu alone, and in any case it may be dangerous."

So that Michael and Saluki had to be content to wait with the Gzendis, standing with downcast eyes a good distance off.

Mr. Jameson found the witch-doctor lying on a rush mat in the semi-darkness. He writhed and groaned. Beads of perspiration stood out on his wrinkled, black face. He cowered against the mat when he saw the missionary approaching and his bloodshot eyes were full of terror.

"Kikembu, I think you know who I am," Mr. Jameson said.

The witch-doctor nodded. He was indeed changed from the man who had danced and with evil speeches led the Gzendis to do the fearful things they had done.

"You come to take revenge," he groaned. "You come to kill me."

Mr. Jameson shook his head slowly. "No, Kikembu," he replied. "Let me first see what is wrong with you and then we will talk."

As the missionary bent to make his examination, the witch-doctor shrieked, sure that now his end was approaching. A quick look over Kikembu assured Mr.

82

Jameson that what he had suspected was right. The man had a dangerous tropical fever. What was more, the fever was extremely catching, and there was an imminent danger that the whole of the Gzendis might be infected—and die.

He took an hypodermic from his bag and bared the witch-doctor's arm. Now Kikembu was sure that he was to die. He let out ear-splitting shrieks of terror.

"This is not going to hurt you," the missionary assured him. "Now—steady—there—it's all over."

Kikembu fell back on to the mat. His eyes rolled in fear. Mr. Jameson hurried to the entrance of the palaver house.

"Michael," he called, "the mystery is cleared up. Kikembu would have died of fever if we had arrived much later. The Gzendis know the danger. That is what they meant by the evil spell, and why they were afraid to come out of their houses. What a good thing you rescued the vaccines from the hospital. Run back to the clearing and fetch them for me. And you, Saluki, round up the whole village. We've got to inoculate everybody before it is too late."

CHAPTER NINE

THE old chief, Bembi, insisted on returning with Michael to Filembu.

"They are my children," he said proudly. "Now I must go."

They found that Saluki, his black face now all smiles, had arranged the African villagers in a long line, and Mr. Jameson sat at an improvised table outside the palaver house. The Gzendis were silent and downcast, ashamed of what they had done, afraid of what might happen to them.

Michael put the vaccines on his father's table.

"Thanks, Michael," Mr. Jameson smiled. He prepared the needle for administering the vaccines. Saluki stood close by to help. "Now, Bembarli," he called. "You are the head man. You shall be first."

Bembarli hung back, trembling.

"Come along, Bembarli," Mr. Jameson urged. "This isn't going to hurt you. It'll do you good."

Still Bembarli cowered and his teeth chattered.

"You punish me, Mr. Jameson," he moaned. "You punish all the Gzendis like you punish Kikembu."

Mr. Jameson smiled gently. "So that's it. No, Bembarli. You have got it all wrong. Didn't I say that I would not harm you. Look, this is my son, Michael. You know him?"

Bembarli nodded his head.

"Bare your arm, Michael," Mr. Jameson whispered. "You'll have to be inoculated too, so it's better that you're done first."

Before the wondering gaze of the Gzendis, Mr. Jameson gave the first inoculation to his son.

Michael smiled round at them.

"See, it's all right," he cried out. "Didn't hurt a bit."

Bembarli stumbled forward, his arm outstretched.

"You do it to your son. Then it all right," he exclaimed. "Please do it to me."

After that there was no difficulty. The Gzendis came one by one, smiles of relief on their faces, to be treated.

And when it was all over Mr. Jameson gathered them all before him and spoke to them.

"There have been evil things done in Filembu," he said. "You have listened to the voice of Kikembu, as Bembarli said. You have been mad. See, the school, the chapel and the hospital that we built have gone. And other worse things might have happened. I am very sad."

Groans came from the assembled Gzendis. Bembarli stepped forward.

"We are sad too, Mr. Jameson," he said. "The madness is gone. Will you forgive us?"

"Listen, Gzendis," Mr. Jameson went on. "When I came back you were hiding in your huts. You thought that Kikembu had put his magic on the village, and when you saw me you were sure that I was going to punish you for your wrong-doing. You would not let me give you the medicine to keep away the sickness of Kikembu, would you?"

They hung their heads. "We deserved to be punished, Mr. Jameson," Bembarli said honestly. "We were afraid."

"Yes," Mr. Jameson nodded his head, "you did deserve to be punished, but because I worship and love God, I had not to punish you, but to bring you help. I had to forgive you because God will forgive you if you are really sorry and try never again to be led into evil ways."

"But, Mr. Jameson," Bembarli stammered. "how will God forgive us. We do much evil."

"Let me tell you about Effendi," Mr. Jameson explained. "He lived in Goez. Many of you know him. He rescued us and came with us into the jungle. There he was bitten by a snake and would have died. He knew we must get to Filembu, and he hid himself to die so that we should not be delayed. Wasn't that a brave thing?"

The Gzendis all nodded their heads in agreement.

"Yes, he would have given up his life for us," Mr. Jameson said. "And God sent His Son into the world. There were men just like you, who listened to evil talk, and they killed Him. He died. You see, Gzendis, He gave up His life as Effendi was prepared to do, because He loved everybody and because we had done wicked things. And because Jesus died, He suffered for all our evil, and thus God can forgive us. His Son was punished for us. Do you see that, Gzendis?"

There was a long, bewildered silence, and then a sudden cry and Kikembu came staggering through the crowd. He fell in front of Mr. Jameson's table.

"I listen, Mr. Jameson," he gasped. "I evil man. I

86

plan to kill you and make trouble for white man. I do many wicked things. You come to Filembu and I expect you to kill me.''

He fell full length, panting. Mr. Jameson rushed forward and lifted his head gently.

"You were kind to me." Kikembu smiled. "You not kill me. You different. You saved my life. God different if He make men like you. He forgive, you say. You told the Gzendis so. He forgive because Jesus died. Tell me, Mr. Jameson, did Jesus die for old Kikembu, the witch-doctor, too?''

"Yes," Mr. Jameson replied quietly. "He died for Kikembu too."

"Then will you talk to God for me?" Kikembu pleaded.

Very quietly, Mr. Jameson prayed with the old witch-doctor, and slowly a smile spread over Kikembu's face.

"I feel it," he gasped. "I feel here in my heart. I feel good. I feel God forgive me. I no longer be evil man. I tell men at Goez to go. I help build new hospital and chapel. I, Kikembu, will try to be Christian."

All the Gzendis knelt down then in prayer, and this time they really understood what they were doing.

The evil that had beset Filembu was over. Now was to begin the rebuilding and putting everything into order again. But thanks were due to God for His deliverance. Now the Gzendis recovered their joy and laughter, and with a will they set about their new tasks.

A few days later, before them all, Kikembu burnt his mask and all the paraphernalia of his witchcraft. "I,

Kikembu," he declared, "am no longer witch-doctor. I follow true God."

And, standing a little way off, the old chief, Bembi, put his arm round Michael's shoulder.

"The drums, my son," he murmured. "Brought evil to my children. God has brought love and peace. Bembi will die content."